Susie Q's Kids Positive Reflections
Good Characteristics

Written by **Dr. Mary Welsh**
Illustrated by **Gabby Correia**

This book belongs to

_____

Susie Q's Kids Positive Reflections
My Special Angel

Susie "Q" McBride-Welsh

Angel Susie helps you understand grief. Get your copy today.

Published by Author Academy Elite
PO Box 43, Powell, OH 43035
www.AuthorAcademyElite.com

Susie Q's Kids Positive Reflections:
Good Characteristics coloring book

Identifiers:
ISBN: 978-1-64746-296-3 (paperback)

Available in paperback.

Written by Dr. Mary Welsh
Illustrated by Gabby Correia

Susie McBride-Welsh

This book is dedicated to Aunt Susie, a Special Angel and one Terrific Aunt.

We Love You!

Parents learn more about the
Power of Positivity.

Teach your children to lead positive and
purposeful lives following
the Four Aspects of Positive Reflection

REMEMBER -
understand your past and
cherish your memories

REFLECT -
look at how your past and
present impact your life

RECREATE -
create a 'new you', a 'new normal' in your
situation and look for the power of positivity

RELATE -
embrace your 'new you' in all that you
do, help and support others, and
give back in our community

drmarywelsh.com

We started Susie Q's Kids,
a 501c3 non-profit,
to brighten and inspire the
lives of children and young adults
with distribution of our comfort bags
to kids in hospitals, shelters,
foster care, grieving, and others.

To learn more, visit:

susieqskids.org
drmary@susieqskids.org

Read her adult grief book:
Journey into the looking Glass:
Finding Hope After the Loss of Loved Ones

Dr. Mary Welsh
drmarywelsh.com

You are amazing

You are the best

It feels good to care

You can do anything

Count on each other

CONSIDERATE

Care for others

DEPENDABLE

Do your best to help

ENCOURAGING

Everyone is special

Share with your friends

Have fun together

Enjoy your friends

GENEROUS

Give to others

Be generous

Help with a smile

helpful

Lend a hand

Lying hurts

Look for cool ideas

Jokes are fun

Know others care

Learning is fun

Love your family

Friends for life

MOTIVATED

It is more fun together

Never forget to smile

Clean your own room

Take turns playing

Please be kind

You have the power

Pretty cool, nice job

Quit playing and help

RELIABLE

Read lots of books

Be a good role model

Share your feelings

Special buddies share

Sisters are goofy

Show your strength

Smile and help

Treat each other nice

THOUGHTFUL

Say thank you

Take a leap

Build it up together

Use together

Positive vibes

Way to go

X MARKS THE SPOT

eXtra special

You are awesome

Zany play

Thank you for coloring, sending good wishes to you

Love Susie Q

Made in the USA
Monee, IL
22 June 2023

36611645R10033